C000271449

Melting Point

Written by Marcus Sabom

Text copyright 2019 by Marcus Sabom

All rights reserved. Except as permitted under the U.S. Copyright Act of 1976, no part of this publication may be reproduced, distributed, or transmitted in any form or by any means, or stored in a database or retrieval system, without the prior written permission of the writer.

Marcus Sabom
10718 Grand Pines Dr.
Sugar Land, TX 77498
www.amazon.com/author/marcussabom

First Paperback Edition: June 2019

The characters and events portrayed in this book are fictitious. Any similarity to real persons, living or dead, is coincidental and not intended by the author.

Sabom, Marcus, 1983-
Melting Point : a novelette / by Marcus Sabom – 1st ed.

Summary: Chris and his old friend John reconnect during a hot summer in Houston, Texas. While Chris waits for the AC at his home to get fixed, he starts seeing demons with red eyes following him, threatening those he loves.

ISBN: 9781073066148

{1. Horror - Fiction. 2. Thriller - Fiction. 3. Suspense - Fiction. 4. Drama - Fiction.}

Printed in the United States of America

Dedication:

This story is dedicated to the inventor of air conditioning. We wouldn't survive these hot summers without your wonderful gift.

Also, to my editor, Rebecca Torrellas. Thanks for making sure my shoes are tied and my shirt tucked in.

And, as always, to you, dear reader. I recommend reading this story with a cool breeze and a glass of your favorite chilled beverage.

I hope you enjoy it!

Table of Contents

Marcus Sabom's
horror, suspense, thriller

The Good
Friend

is available on Amazon.com

Follow Marcus on his Amazon page
http://www.amazon.com/author/marcussabom
for upcoming books, book trailers and more!

Look for the book series:
A Fairies' Tale
Created by Rebecca Torrellas

In Love There's War

On Broken Wings *(by Marcus Sabom)*

Tangled Webs

Awakened Fire

For a list of all published and upcoming books in this series, visit the official website:
www.afairiestaleseries.com

Chapter 1

    To say it was hot outside would be an understatement and repetitive. Of course, it was hot — it was the middle of summer in Houston, Texas. If it were anything other than hot, climatologists would be pulling out their hair trying to figure out why. The moment you walked outside for any reason, you started sweating. It didn't matter if you stood in the shade making the least amount of effort possible, you sweated.

    Which is precisely what Chris Kohen was doing as he sat in the shade on his front porch at five in the early evening wearing a pair of blue gym shorts and that's it, too hot for any more clothing. Chris was a well-built, 6'3", olive-skinned guy with a five o'clock shadow decorating his chiseled jaw. With his sandy blonde hair and brown eyes, if he smiled, he looked like a model. It was his good looks that earned him the nickname of "pretty boy" with the construction crew with whom he worked.

However, right now, he sure as hell didn't feel like smiling. He had enough motivation to sip his sweet iced tea and that was it. He would often fantasize about being one of those winter Texans who had a house somewhere up north for the summer. Alas, carrying out such a fantasy was for someone who was rich and didn't have to work, so he settled for his iced tea.

Chris looked around his little suburb neighborhood. He lived near Interstate 10, close to the Heights in a one-story wooden house. Nothing was happening, save the one brave lady doing her daily jogging no matter what the temperature was. Some cars were passing by on the street. He heard a dog barking off in the distance as well as the nearby sounds of traffic.

In his next door neighbor's backyard, their dog was outside panting away. He looked at the dog's water bowl. It looked empty. Feeling bad for the poor thing, Chris went inside, filled up the biggest cup he could find with water, came back outside and — reaching over the neighbor's waist-high chain link fence — dumped the water into the bowl. The dog got up and starting drinking. Chris gave the dog a lazy salute and went back to his porch where the shade was.

As he continued to look around out of boredom, the sight of a shape wearing a long, black cloak standing in a neighbor's window caught his eye. Even though the sun was shining bright, the form was still blacker than the night sky and seemed to swallow up the light around it. Chris couldn't make out a face or any discernible features; the only thing he saw was two glowing red eyes. The eyes had no features, no iris, no pupils, just a red glow coming out of two thin oval-shaped slits, and yet he knew those red eyes were staring right at him.

He felt his heart start to race. His insides ran cold. It seemed to be standing inside, yet the shadowy cloak it was wearing seemed to billow and wave as if reacting to a strong wind. Even if it was outside, there was no wind at all. The air was still and thick with humidity. This isn't real, he tried telling himself. The sharp sting of salty sweat made him snap his eyes shut.

He wiped the sweat away and looked again. The shape seemed to have disappeared. He stared at the window for a good few minutes waiting for... whatever it was to come back. It didn't. Chris shook his head and downed the rest of his iced tea in three big gulps. This god damned heat was getting to him, making him see things. Of course, there wasn't a malevolent shadow across the street. At least that's what he told himself, and he almost believed it.

Just then his wife, Lucy, pulled her Honda Accord next to his Chevrolet truck. After taking a minute or so to make sure she had everything, she took off her sunglasses, turned off her car, got out and headed toward the house dressed in her uniform of medical scrubs after pulling a shift at M.D. Anderson hospital.

"Babe, what are you doing out here?" Lucy asked as she continued her walk to the house.

"Would you believe it's cooler out here than it is in there?"

Chris responded.

"AC guy didn't come yet?"

"Said they were backed up on work, lots of AC units going out, I guess. Can't imagine why," Chris said, his sarcasm evident. "Should be here tomorrow though."

"C'mon, I'll get dinner ready."

"Tell me you're freezing soup and serving it like a popsicle."

Lucy chuckled a bit at that, "Close, it's Greek pasta salad, straight from the fridge."

"Good enough."

Chris followed Lucy inside and, sure enough, a thick blanket of hot air enveloped the two as they walked in. Lucy went to the bedroom to change out of her scrubs and take one of her daily birth control pills while Chris started opening up windows and turning on fans. When he finished, he poured himself another big glass of sweet iced tea and poured Lucy one as well.

He sat down on his couch in the living room where pictures of him and Lucy together, including some wedding photos, were hung on the wall along with some artwork. A gun rack with two hunting rifles and a shotgun safely locked in place decorated the wall as well. There was ammunition in the small hallway table underneath the guns.

Out of curiosity, Chris flipped to the news. Must be a slow day; all they could talk about was the weather.

"So Dave, think this heat will let up anytime soon?" the news anchor asked the meteorologist, her voice nauseatingly pleasant, as the camera cut to an older man dressed in a suit, his hair perfectly styled, his face not sweating at all.

"Well, Michelle, unfortunately, not anytime soon. This is a particularly aggressive heat wave, and it's here to stay for the foreseeable future. Already we've experienced record-high temperatures today because of this high-pressure system sitting right on top of us, and the rest of the week looks to be more of the same."

Chris turned off the TV. Tell me something I don't fucking know already, he thought to himself. Lucy came out with two bowls of pasta salad wearing nothing but underwear and a midriff tank top. Chris couldn't help but admire his beautiful wife with her shoulder-length, strawberry-blonde hair, creamy skin with tattoos decorating various spots on her body. She had big brown eyes and a voluptuous figure. Sometimes, just for fun, Lucy would do a photo shoot with a local photographer.

"Well, that's one good thing about this weather," he said, giving her an amorous look.

Lucy rolled her eyes as she sat down next to him.

"Oh yeah, I feel so sexy sweating like a pig," she said.

"Well, actually," Chris stretched out the 'actually,' knowing she hated it when he said those words. "Pigs don't sweat. That's why they roll around in the mud; it's what keeps them cool."

"Shut up and eat your salad, mansplainer," Lucy said while handing him a bowl.

Chris chuckled a bit as they started eating. Lucy rolled her eyes but couldn't help but smile a bit. The cold salad did feel good to eat.

"So, how was work?" he asked in between bites.

"The usual, chemo treatments, cleaning up bodily fluids, fun times. You?"

"Miserable. Fucking foreman gets to sit in his nice air-conditioned office while us grunts sweat away on steel beams. It's a wonder none of us have had a heat stroke yet."

"Y'all have access to water and shade, right?"

"Yeah, we do. Even so, I feel like the wicked witch of the west out there," he said. "I'm meeellltttiinnnggg! Meeeellllttttiiiinnnggg!"

Lucy giggled a bit, and the pair continued eating.

Chapter 2

As Chris was in his truck, battling traffic on his way to another day of steel beams and pneumatic drills, Officer John Harold knelt in front of a tombstone. The words "In Loving Memory of Gerald Warner. He died a hero" etched into the stone. He lay a bouquet of flowers in front of the tombstone. He wasn't in uniform; that would come later. For right now, he was in regular civilian street clothes. He wiped the sweat from his brow as he stood up.

"I'm sorry, Gerald," he said to the headstone.

As he walked out of the cemetery, his mind flooded with the memories of when Gerald was alive, riding in the patrol car next to him. The two of them would be laughing about whatever nonsense Gerald would look up on his phone while John drove around. Then the inevitable memory would surface.

It hadn't even been a month when the two of them pulled over a person driving recklessly. As John ran the plates, Gerald got out and headed to the driver's window to get his license. That's when the driver ambushed Gerald with a gun and pulled the trigger before either of them could react. John called it in as fast as he could while getting out of his car to give first aid to his partner.

By the time the ambulance was able to clear the gridlocked Houston traffic, it was too late. The driver was apprehended within an hour. The guy burst from his car all crazy-eyed and waving his gun around, screaming something about a red-eyed shadow demon. Mere seconds later his fellow officers were announcing that the "suspect was down" over the radio. It would be revealed later the guy had a long history of psychotic episodes and violent outbursts.

John couldn't help but blame himself for his partner's death. It was only after Gerald had gotten out of the car that the info on the license plate would have warned them. By then, it was too late. It no longer mattered if the suspect was in custody or in the ground. It didn't change what happened.

Standing at 5'10" and an athletic 160 lbs., his dark brown skin, black curly hair, and boyish features didn't help as far making him seem authoritative. But he worked out relentlessly and studied various martial art disciplines, including Brazilian jiu-jitsu and krav maga, as well as practiced shooting his gun. He was determined never to let what happened to his partner occur to anyone else, not if he could help it. These were the thoughts he conveyed to his psychologist an hour after visiting the cemetery during his mandatory therapy.

As the therapist jotted down her notes, she asked John a surprising question, "Do you contemplate suicide?"

John was taken aback by that question, but upon introspection, he had to admit it did cross his mind. Gerald's death had filled him with feelings of inadequacy, powerlessness, and a deep depression came over him. Even while training, he was always haunted by the feeling of "this won't be enough," which propelled him forward, but never let him be satisfied. In the dead of night, those feelings would overwhelm him, and the thought of just putting himself out of his misery didn't seem so bad.

But then he'd look over to see his husband sleeping next to him. He had met Clyde while in the police academy. Clyde was in school to become a teacher. Clyde's mocha colored skin, brown wavy hair, full beard he kept trimmed and neat, at 6'2", and slender with a cute ass. How could John not want to get his phone number? It wasn't long before the two realized how compatible they were as people as well. Falling in love with each other was easy.

It was that love that sustained John after his police partner was killed. Through it all, his husband Clyde had been a rock. Making sure he ate, crying with him, knowing when to give space, and knowing when to be there. Clyde was the only thing in John's life that made any sense right now. It was that knowledge that allowed him to respond to the therapist's question.

"Sometimes, but nothing serious. I don't want to do it

anyway."

"Why not?"

"Because I care too much. My husband, those I work with, they depend on me. I can't handle facing them as a failure again."

"But sometimes things happen that are beyond our control."

That was something repeated ad nauseam by many people to him. Part of him knew it was true, but it was just something the rest of him couldn't quite accept.

"I know, but I can't help it if I keep thinking, maybe if I had done something different. If I had just told him to wait..." he trailed off.

"We've all played the 'what if' and 'if only' game. What you're experiencing is normal. However, you can't let it dominate your life," she said.

That was something else John had heard a lot.

"I know, I'm trying. This has been helping. Really."

"I'm glad to hear it. Before we conclude our session, I have some homework for you. I would like for you to start reconnecting with people. Friends or some family members that you haven't spoken to in a while. I think it'll be good for you to focus on what you have rather than what you lost."

John thought about that for a bit. It seemed like good advice.

"Okay, I'll do that. Thanks, doc."

Chapter 3

After another long day in the unbearable heat, Chris was heading home. At least the AC in Chris's truck worked just fine. He hoped the AC in his house would be repaired as well. In the meantime, he was determined to make the most of his temporary oasis from the heat in his truck.

As he came to a stop, he noticed in the car in front of him a small child looking at him. He wondered why the kid wasn't wearing a seatbelt but gave the child a friendly wave anyway. Out of habit, he glanced in his rearview mirror. That's when he noticed the driver behind him was staring at him with bright red glowing eyes — the same glowing red eyes the shape in the window had yesterday.

He looked away and shook his head. He was driving home facing the setting sun, and it was affecting his vision, at least that's what he told himself. He faced forward only to see the small child he waved at earlier now glaring at him with glowing red eyes. Chris scrunched his eyes closed and tried to steady his breathing. He could feel his heart trying to burst through his chest. What was happening? There was no way any of this was real!

The sound of an impatient car horn startled him. His eyes opened and saw an empty road ahead of him and a green light. The car behind him blasted their horn again.

"Alright! Alright! Calm the fuck down!" Chris shouted, knowing the other driver couldn't hear him.

Chris stepped on the gas and took off. As much as he tried to take deep breaths and calm himself, it wasn't working. Chris saw the entrance to a suburban neighborhood and pulled into it. He found an empty stretch of the curb and parked there. This was twice now he saw something. What did it mean?

Was he seeing things? Was he having delusions or was something after him? Revealing itself a little at a time, toying with him, was Chris's destiny already decided by this force? No, that can't be it. That's ridiculous. People claim to see Jesus in pieces of toast or on grass stains. It's just their biased projections; their brain trying to make sense out of something that makes no sense.

That's all it was, the sun got in his eyes, and it made him see things. For a moment, his exhausted mind cooked up some story about demons or whatever and gave him a fright to keep him from passing out from heat exhaustion in his truck. Yeah, that was it. It had to be.

But as much as Chris tried to convince himself, that cold drop of fear in the pit of his stomach never left him.

Chris rummaged around his glove compartment for his sunglasses. After putting them on, he was about to head out when someone knocked on his window giving him yet another scare. He glanced over and saw a police officer complete with a hat and large sunglasses staring at him. Chris was pretty sure this wasn't a delusion.

The officer made a "roll down your window" motion. Chris did so. Fucking A, what did he do wrong this time? Chris already started making mental calculations as to how much he was about to get fined for... doing whatever it was he did.

"May I see your license and insurance information, sir?" the cop asked in a deep voice.

Chris handed over the necessary information. It was like getting blood drawn, just stare straight ahead, think about something else, and it's over before you know it.

"Sir, I'm going to need you to step out of the vehicle."

This caught Chris off guard. He wasn't drunk. He was parked. Was his vehicle about to get towed?

"May I ask why, officer?"

That's when John's voice returned to normal, "Because I haven't seen you in forever, shithead."

Chris stared for a moment as John took off his hat and sunglasses, then Chris recognized his childhood friend.

"Holy shit, you asshole!" Chris said with a big smile.

John was too busy laughing to respond, enjoying his prank too much.

"Okay, okay, okay," John said, getting a hold of himself. "I'll make it up to you, let me buy you a drink."

"I thought cops weren't allowed to drink on the job."

"Good thing I'm heading back to the station to clock out. I got the time if you do. Name the place."

Chris was never one to pass up a free drink, "You know where the Sideshow Bar is?"

"Absolutely. I hear they have good hot sauce there."

"You know it, buddy. I'll head there."

"Alright, see you as soon as I can."

John headed back to his cruiser as Chris drove off toward the restaurant. Chris was feeling pretty good about reconnecting with an old friend, so much so he even forgot about the fright he had.

Chapter 4

An hour later, Chris was finishing texting his wife to let her know what he was up to when John joined him at the Sideshow Bar.

"Nice place," John said while sitting down.

Chris had to chuckle at that. It was a horror-themed bar and restaurant. The waiters were all either dressed like Gomez or Morticia Addams. The walls were decorated with posters and art of horror monsters of all types, from classic monsters to modern-day ghosts and slashers. A source of entertainment was the sign by the front door that said, "This isn't Disney World, assholes don't get free shit."

Chris wasn't much for horror films. He preferred high-octane action movies himself, but this place served the best Italian food he'd ever had, and Chris could never say no to the lasagna, linguine and fried spaghetti served here. They also served some amazing appetizers and a wide array of homemade hot sauces. From mild and tangy to holy shit, someone call an ambulance and every flavor and heat level in between. All the hot sauces had horror-themed names like Vamp Slayer Roasted Garlic, Bearded Lady habañero, and Tortured Souls jalapeño and tomatillo sauce.

"Just wait until you try the food here," Chris said.

Their server came by and took their drink orders. They both agreed to a shot of Jack Daniels to start, a pitcher of Texas Thunder Light beer, and then soda for the remainder of the evening. A few minutes later they clinked their shot glasses and toasted to seeing old friends. It wasn't long before they started reminiscing about shared memories.

"You remember when you pushed Tyrone Jacobson's sister into the mud? You had to hide at my house when he was looking to beat your ass," John chuckled.

"Oh shit, yeah. Not my bravest moment," Chris said.

"To be fair, you did deserve an ass whooping."

"Yeah, I was a little shit back then. But, c'mon, she wouldn't stop singing that "Merry Old Land of Oz" song from Wizard of Oz. It drove me nuts!"

Both John and Chris cracked up laughing.

"Hey, at least you're no longer a little shit," John said.

"Oh, I don't know, my wife might say differently if you ask her," Chris said.

"I'd love to, when do I get to meet her?"

"I'll chat with her tonight, what about you? Got a wife?"

John figured this was coming. He braced himself and told Chris about his husband, Clyde. To John's surprise and relief, Chris took it in stride.

"Hey, we all have to be something, right?" Chris said.

"True, but thanks anyway for not freaking out."

"It's all good, my friend. It's been too long. We lost contact, and I wasn't even sure if you were still in town."

"I wasn't for a while, but then I finally got the station transfer I wanted. So now I'm back home."

"What about your better half, is he happy here?"

"It's taken some getting used to, but Clyde is finding his own life here."

"So tell me about him. How you two met; all that."

As John began to wax poetic about his husband, Chris's attention drifted toward the shape he saw in the neighbor's window on the other side of the restaurant. It was the same. It had to be. The same shimmering billowing blackness. Could nobody else see it? He watched wait staff and customers walk right by it as if nothing was there.

As if it knew it had Chris's attention, Chris saw it rotate until those same glowing red eyes began staring at him. Chris felt it beckon him. It didn't move. It didn't have to. Chris just knew it wanted him. What for? He didn't know, and he didn't want to find out. Yet he felt paralyzed, compelled to remain still to await his fate. Chris's heart raced. He felt sweat beading on his forehead and his breathing rapid.

The shape knew Chris was afraid, and it seemed to enjoy it.

That's when John grabbed Chris's arm, startling the hell out of him.

"Hey, whoa, whoa, you okay?" John asked.

Chris looked around, and the shape was gone.

"Yeah... yeah, sorry, I..."

"What happened man? You look like you saw a ghost."

John looked behind him at the spot where Chris was staring and saw a reprinted image from the "Scary Stories to Tell in the Dark" featuring a ghastly image staring at the customers.

"Was that it?" John asked, referring to the image.

Chris looked again and saw the same image. The image was across the room. No, not again. He was trying to enjoy dinner and drinks with his friend. Why was this happening now? It couldn't have been a heat-induced delusion, the restaurant's AC was working great. But then he had felt hot when he saw the... no, no, nothing was there!

That's when he saw John's worried look on his face. He didn't want John worrying about him. All his life, he had been told not to be a burden on anyone and to deal with his own problems like a man. Now he was bringing down the evening. His mind scrambled to come up with something that would alleviate John's concerns.

"Yeah, wow, that hot sauce they give you with the chips hit me harder than I thought," Chris said, forcing a chuckle.

John wasn't convinced.

"Yeah, it's got some kick, but... dude, seriously, you were

freaking out. What's going on?"

Chris was getting desperate; then he had an idea.

"Okay, I thought I saw an old girlfriend who tried to pull some baby daddy shit on me. It turned out she got knocked up by someone else, but even so, not someone I wanted to see, you know? Wasn't her, just one of the waitresses looked a lot like her."

John seemed to accept it, not completely, but enough.

"Okay man, as long as you're alright."

Chris was saved by their food arriving, and the two began eating. It didn't take long for John to figure out why Chris loved the food at the place so much. By the time they were finished eating, Chris's scare had been forgotten. That's when John checked his phone.

"Damn, it's later than I thought. It's past my bedtime."

"Yeah, it's a school night for both of us. But, hey, if you're still serious about getting together again, I'll chat with my honey tonight."

"Sounds great, I'll do the same. Here's my number. Let me know what evenings work for you," John said as he gave Chris one of his professional cards.

John insisted on paying the check, so Chris left a generous tip. They exchanged a hug and headed to their respective vehicles. As Chris drove home, the truck's AC going full force, the recent memory of having yet another vision crept back into his head. Again, he told himself it was just this fucking heat getting the better of him. Again, he told himself it was nothing. Again, he told himself not to make a big deal out of it.

Chris pulled into his driveway and saw the living room lights on and, to his chagrin, the windows all open. Which meant the god damn AC guy didn't come today either. Sure enough, a wet blanket made of hot thick air greeted him when he walked in the door. He saw Lucy sitting on the couch, dressed in her usual "it's way too hot to wear clothes" outfit of underwear and a midriff tank top, watching TV. She looked over at him when he walked in.

"Hey, how was dinner with your friend?" she asked.

"Good, he wants to get together again. Want to tag along?"

"Sure, he can tell me humiliating stories from when you were a kid."

He chuckled a bit. His wife always did have a mischievous sense of humor. It was one of the things he loved about her.

"So do we have a free evening anytime soon?"

"Fuck, how about tomorrow? It'll get us out of this hot ass house," she responded.

Chris couldn't argue with that logic. He took out the card John gave him and started texting his friend.

Chapter 5

The next day, Chris pulled into his driveway after another hard day's work in the hot sun. He sat in his truck for a bit, trying to soak up as much air conditioning as he could before going into his house. The AC company still hadn't sent someone out. Chris had half a mind just to buy a new AC unit from a different company and tell his current one to get fucked. The extended warranty he paid for with his current one was starting to become not worth the fucking hassle.

Chris sent a text to John telling him he and his wife would see him tonight. A minute later, John sent a thumbs up emoji back as a response. Chris then sighed the beleaguered sigh of a man who knew he had to go inside his stuffy, hot house. He wondered what the point of even taking a shower was if he was going to start sweating the moment he got out of the shower. Maybe if he took a cold shower?

He turned off his truck and headed inside, already sweating from the short walk from the driveway to the front door. He unlocked his door and, like clockwork, was greeted by the familiar yet unwelcome wet blanket of thick hot air.

It seemed hotter than usual too. Chris expected the hot air, but this was overwhelming and stifling. The thick air was making it difficult to breathe. This was too much. He started to pull his cellphone out of his pocket. Some repairer needed to get their ass down here now! He started dialing, but the sweat dripped into his eyes. He clenched his eyes shut, trying to drown out the stinging sensation.

He started feeling dizzy. He opened his eyes, trying to find something to hang on to. But the sweat was still blurring his vision. He felt his heart beating faster as he broke out into a cold, clammy sweat. He thought at any moment he was going to throw up. However, the last thing he saw was the floor of his house rushing toward him.

The sound of thunder rattling the house startled Chris. He opened his eyes and looked around. How long was he out? He checked his phone, only a minute or so. He must have fainted. How fucking hot was it? Now it was raining? There wasn't a cloud in the sky all day and no mention of this on the news. When did this happen? There was the old joke of "Don't like the weather in Houston? Wait an hour," but this was beyond even that.

Chris picked himself off the floor to head to the living room. Maybe the weatherman was trying to explain where this storm originated. As he stood up and steadied himself, the sound of a floorboard creek sent a chill down his spine. Was someone here? This was an old house, it's not like creeks and groans weren't part of the package, but Chris knew the sound of someone stepping on a floorboard.

"Lucy? You home?" he called out.

No answer. Was there a thief in the house? Chris glanced toward the rifles on the living room wall. He wondered how fast he could get his shotgun unlocked. He knew he'd have a hard time shooting someone; he wasn't a violent person. But he also knew the sound of a shotgun cocking was an all too familiar sound and would often send even the most daring soul scurrying away.

That's when he heard the unmistakable sound of a child giggling. He breathed a sigh of relief — just some neighborhood kid pulling some kind of a prank. The sound came from the kitchen. He knew it was raining outside, but still, if the kid felt okay about being cute during a storm, then surely whoever it was wouldn't be bothered by the rain — time for the kid to go.

He looked down the hallway that led to the kitchen. It was dark in there. The storm was making everything dark, and he hadn't turned any lights on yet.

"Okay kid, the joke's over. Time to go home!"

He expected at any moment to see a small child dart out the back door. Instead, the hallway got darker and darker as if pure blackness was swallowing the kitchen and pouring through the hallway. Chris stood there frozen, his mind refusing to comprehend what he was seeing. Those two red eyes appeared in the black, the red eyes that have been staring at him since the other day. Those red eyes were pulling him toward them.

The primitive part of Chris's brain took over. He had seen all he needed to see. He'd make sense of it later, right now, all he knew was he needed to get away. He darted for his bedroom, pulled open the drawer in his nightstand and pulled out a small handgun. It was Lucy's gun, but now was not the time to worry about that.

He flattened himself against the wall by the door. He wasn't sure if a gun would do anything to those red eyes, but he had to try something. He then remembered some crap about a story about a killer clown that fed on fear. Okay, well, maybe if he showed... whatever the fuck that was he wasn't afraid, it would fuck off.

Chris summoned whatever courage he could and yelled, "Okay asshole! Whoever you are, I got a gun. I'll blow your fucking head off. Get out of my house!"

Chris waited with bated breath. He listened for any sound, keeping his eyes peeled for any movement. He waited. Nothing happened; just the sound of rain and the occasional flash of lightning and thunder. Maybe it worked. Maybe his show of bravado actually worked. Chris slowly, as steady as possible, peered out of his doorway into the hallway. A little bit at a time, prepared at any moment to see something he didn't want to see and yank himself back into his bedroom.

He saw nothing. He was about to let out the breath he didn't realize he was holding when the sound of footsteps running on his roof jerked his attention up. The steps went from one side of his bedroom to the wall facing away from the door. Someone was fucking with him, that had to be it! This was just an elaborate prank, probably some of his buddies from the construction crew trying to pull a fast one on him. It was the only thing that made any sort of sense.

He heard another floorboard creek outside his bedroom door. If this was a prank, someone was going to be sorry. There were harmless pranks, and then there was this. Whoever was doing this was downright sadistic! But then, despite telling himself this was just a ruse, Chris knew better. Chris knew he was being toyed with by a dark force that was beyond his comprehension. He felt so helpless, so small, so insignificant.

He had to look, though. He knew he had to despite every fiber in his being screaming at him not to. Once again, he leaned out of the bedroom. Slow and steady, at any moment prepared to dart back in. There was a window in his bedroom; he was confident he could crash through it if he needed to. He inched out... bit by bit... and once again saw nothing.

He sagged against the wall in his bedroom still facing the empty hallway. There was no evil entity, no shadow demon. He was going crazy. He was seeing things. Was the heat making him delusional? He supposed it didn't matter. The result was the result. He had saved up enough money, he could afford to take time off work to get his head straight. He'd have to find a place that took his insurance, but he knew it would be a pain in the ass to find though. Maybe Lucy could help out; she was a nurse, and she must know some people to call.

Chris felt a tingle starting at the top of his spine. He felt that tingle work its way down his back like a drop of icy water. He felt every hair on his body stand straight up. He felt eyes like fire searing a hole into his back. Don't turn around; don't turn around! Just run, the hallway is empty, just go, don't stop until you're out the door! Despite Chris trying to command himself to listen, he found himself turning around, compelled to face the thing he knew was behind him.

He didn't know how it got there. However, as he turned, there it was — the billowing shadowy form, the red eyes piercing through its unnatural darkness. The shape lunged at him with blinding speed. Chris managed to swing his arm around to fire a shot at the being, but it had no effect.

Before he knew it, Chris was on the ground, the being inches from his face. Chris tried to fight, but when his hands contacted the creature, it felt like ice cold acid. He heard the being scream. It sounded like every ear-piercing sound reverberating through his mind. Chris screamed in pain and fear as the monster seemed to peer into his very soul. Claiming all it saw as its own. In the shadowy form, Chris saw an abyss containing everything and nothing at all.

Chapter 6

The sound of a door slamming snapped Chris out of the nightmare he was having. He awoke where he had fainted, drenched in his sweat. It was daylight, no storm, no shape. He looked around like a frightened animal, searching for any hint of danger, the smallest sign of trouble. He heard footsteps moving around in the other room.

"Who's there?" he demanded.

"It's just me, honey," came Lucy's voice from the other room.

Chris gave a slight sigh of relief, but still didn't completely trust himself yet. What if the shape was imitating Lucy's voice as another way of tormenting him? Chris relaxed in full when he saw Lucy come around the corner, still wearing her work scrubs. Her face became one of concern when she saw him on the floor, leaning against the wall.

"Babe, are you okay?" She asked as she knelt in front of him and put the back of her hand on his forehead.

It was just a bad dream, he kept telling himself. Just a stupid, lucid dream that felt a little too real, but now it was over.

"I'm fine, I promise."

"You don't look fine, not at all."

"It's too fucking hot, that's all," Chris said as he started picking himself up.

When he finished standing up, he tried to give Lucy a reassuring smile. He could tell she wasn't buying it.

"Maybe we should stay home tonight," she said.

"No, let's go somewhere where there's air conditioning."

Lucy stood there with a fixed look on her face. It was a look Chris was all too familiar with. She had already made up her mind about something, and there was little anyone could do or say that was going to convince her otherwise. He knew she had made up her mind that he wasn't feeling well; she was a nurse, and it was her job to know these things. But he also knew he wanted to get out of the house and see his friend.

"Tell you what; I'll go take a cold shower and cool off. C'mon Lucy, don't tell me you want to stay in this sweatbox."

Lucy wiped some sweat from her brow and sighed resignation and said, "Fine, but I reserve the right to take you to a hospital at any point I see fit."

"Deal."

Chris headed to the bathroom while taking off his clothes. As promised, he stepped into his spacious walk-in shower and turned on the cold water nozzle. It took a few moments to get used to the cold water, but it wasn't long before Chris was washing himself like it was any other warm shower.

"I'm coming in," Lucy announced as she stepped into the shower.

Chris stood to the side to give her some room. Much like Chris, it took her a bit to acclimate to the cold water. Chris couldn't help but enjoy the show. It was a show he had seen many times, and he never got tired of it. He had a beautiful wife who was standing in front of him naked and soaking wet. He felt some familiar desires stirring within him.

"Could you get my back?" she asked.

Chris squirted some body wash in his hand and starting soaping up her back. He couldn't help himself and gave her ass a gentle squeeze as well. After the nightmare he had, he could use some pleasure in his life.

"Not now, don't we have to be somewhere soon?" she gently admonished.

Chris kissed her neck and shoulders and wrapped his arms around her. He felt her arch her back a bit. "They can wait."

"And you can't, huh?" Lucy said.

Chris heard her voice getting breathy and softer. He couldn't help but smile a bit as his wife gave all the signs of being turned on as well.

"Nope, can you?"

She kissed his arms as a reply. He started massaging one of her breasts with his hand as he continued to kiss her neck and shoulder. He could feel her breathing start to increase, hear her soft moans. He became hungry for her, and she for him. The water may have been cold, but that wasn't stopping anyone.

She put her hands against the shower wall to steady herself as Chris's lips continued their exploration of her back. He worked his down her back and, when he was kneeling, turned her around. He lifted a leg and put it over his shoulder. He let his tongue and lips continue exploring the inside of her thigh. He felt her hand on his head, guiding him toward her center. He didn't disobey. Lucy cried out in pleasure as Chris knew just where to kiss, just how to lick, just what to do with his fingers to bring her to a climax.

He stood up and kissed her. She pressed her body to his. She pushed away enough to start kissing his body while running her hands up and down his well-defined chest and abs. Chris enjoyed every moment of his wife pleasuring him. He closed his eyes as he felt her hand stroking his erection. She knew how to keep him going just enough, yet another thing to add to the long list of reasons why he loved her.

He reached down and lifted one of her legs. Lucy wrapped an arm around his neck. She reached down with her free hand and guided him into her. She wrapped her other leg around his waist and held onto him as held her up. They both stood there for just a moment, kissing each other, just enjoying the feeling of being together.

Then Lucy started rocking her hips. Slowly, at first, then picking up speed and intensity. The two lovers both moaned in pleasure as Lucy kept up her movements. Lucy's moans and heavy breathing in his ear, her hips moving, Chris could have sworn he was in heaven. He could feel himself get closer and closer. He felt the release, and they both gave a loud moan. He held her up for a few more seconds then let her down, both of them breathing heavy. They gave each other some tender kisses.

"We should... uh... get going soon, I guess," Chris said.

Lucy laughed a bit, "Yeah, probably should."

Chapter 7

The sun was setting when Chris and Lucy pulled up in front of John and Clyde's house. Much like their own, it was a rather unremarkable one story house that was the right size for a loving couple. A few moments after ringing the doorbell, the two couples exchanged greetings and headed inside. It wasn't long before they were seated at the table with a big spread of spicy Mexican food.

The four dug in. The food was so divine they ate as if they'd never eat again.

"John, this is delicious!" Chris said in between bites.

"I appreciate that, but Clyde here is the master chef," John said.

"Bravo, this is wonderful," Lucy said.

"You sure you didn't miss your calling in life, could have opened your own restaurant instead of being a teacher," Chris said while wiping the sweat from his forehead. The spices were getting to him, but the food was too good not to keep eating.

"And miss out on bratty kids bringing their germs to school for me to be sick all the time? I'd hate not to be a part of that glamour," Clyde said.

"Hey, I know that feeling," Lucy added.

They continued chatting, or rather, everyone except Chris continued. Chris's attention was pulled toward the ceiling of his friend's house. The feeling of dread, the sense of not wanting to but doing it anyway. Those now familiar sensations commanded him once again. The shape seemed to spread out and cover the ceiling like a pulsating black blanket, and yet still those red eyes, those unyielding red eyes stared at him.

The sounds of his wife and friends talking seemed distant like they were coming from a muffled room far away from him. Something about how Clyde and John were considering adopting a child. This seemed trivial to him; unimportant. All he could focus on was how he felt like a cornered rat awaiting certain doom by a hungry feline. In some ways, it felt like an odd blessing, a left-handed favor. At least now it would finally be over. He wouldn't have to be afraid anymore, he hoped so anyway.

That's when the shape began to float down from the ceiling, descending like a gentle cloud. At first, Chris thought it was coming for him, but then he watched as it hovered over John and seemed to disappear into him. He watched as John went from relaxed and smiling to enraged in a split second. John grabbed Clyde's arm, berating him about sharing personal business and slugged him as hard as he could.

Clyde fell to the floor, nose bleeding, staring at John in disbelief. Chris had seen enough. There was no way he was letting this vile being take his friend. He'd beat the spirit out of John if he had to.

"You son of a bitch!" Chris shouted, standing up.

"Chris!" Lucy shouted, grabbing his arm.

Chris looked her, "Tell me you didn't just see that!"

"See what?" she demanded.

Chris looked over to see Clyde and John sitting in their chairs, no blood on Clyde's nose as if nothing happened.

"I... I just saw you hit Clyde..." Chris stammered.

"He has never and would never do such a thing," Clyde said.

Chris sank back into his chair and put his head in his hands.

"Chris, are you sure you're okay?" John asked.

"Okay, honey, we need to go," Lucy said, standing up. "Guys, I am so sorry."

Chris stood up, meek and malleable, there was no fight in him. He knew he had screwed up. He knew he was going nuts. He was certain he was seeing things.

"Yeah... listen, I'm really sorry," he said.

"Lucy, are you sure you don't need anything, do you want me to follow you home?" John asked.

"We'll be fine. Thank you, John, Clyde, and again, so sorry," she said.

Lucy led Chris out the door and into his truck. She put him in the passenger seat, and it wasn't long before she was heading toward a mental health facility.

"Chris, what is going on with you?"

"I... I think I'm seeing things."

"Okay, I'm taking you to a hospital."

"Babe, I'm sorry, can we just go home?"

"Hey, I said I reserve the right to take you to a hospital if I see fit. Right now, I most fucking definitely see fit."

"Sweetheart, I'm not saying I won't go to one. But we need to find one that takes our insurance and isn't a piece of shit scam if one of those even exists. You know we can't afford to just drop me off at any place, too much of a gamble."

Chris knew he'd be better off in a mental health facility, but he also knew he had to think about his bank account, if he'd be able to keep his job at all, and if this was temporary or something more permanent he'd have to deal with. He knew Lucy knew all this too.

"I'm taking you home, and you're going to straight to bed, you have the day off tomorrow, right?" Lucy said with a sigh of resignation.

"Yeah."

"Okay, we're researching facilities. You're getting help as soon as possible."

"Absolutely. I don't want to keep living like this."

As much as she hated to do it, Lucy headed home. On their way home, Lucy stopped at a gas station and bought some bags of ice.

She had an idea from her days of living as cheap as possible while she was still in nursing school. When she got home, she poured the ice into a couple of buckets and placed them by Chris's side of the bed with a fan moving the cool air onto Chris's body. After expressing his heartfelt gratitude, Chris had no trouble getting to sleep.

Chapter 8

It was the early morning as the sun was starting to peak over the tops of the neighborhood houses. It was warm, not too hot. Chris emerged from his front door on his day off wearing a white tank top, gym shorts, and tennis shoes, ready for a morning jog. He didn't often go on jogs; his construction job provided plenty of exercise. Still, today was a great day, so why the hell not? He took a moment to take a deep breath and appreciate the beautiful sunrise. A few seconds later, and his shoes were hitting the sidewalk.

Chris jogged at a brisk pace. Not too fast, just enough to get his heart rate up. As the houses passed by him, he heard birds singing playful songs, traffic already in full swing, and the far off smell of breakfast tacos being cooked. Chris was glad he remembered to put his wallet in his shorts pocket. A breakfast taco was the perfect reward for his morning exercise.

As Chris kept up the pace, a car drove by him. Chris stopped. Where the car had driven by was now a red hot heat streak on the road. The streak pulsed as the air simmered around it. Chris watched as the heat streak slowly faded away until the road was it's normal color like nothing had happened. Chris shook his head and kept jogging.

As he rounded the corner, he saw someone standing in the middle of the sidewalk facing him. Chris felt uneasy but kept jogging, prepared to go around whomever it was. As Chris got closer, he realized the person was John's husband, Clyde. Clyde continued to stand there, perfectly still. It was when Chris got closer that he realized Clyde had a huge grin on his face. Like he just found out he won the lottery and never had to work another day in his life.

Chris stopped jogging and started slowly walking up to him. Clyde never moved, his eyes never broke contact with Chris. In fact, he never even blinked. His smile was locked in place as well. If the heat streak had made Chris uneasy, this was downright nerve-wracking. If it weren't for the sight of him breathing, Chris would have sworn he was looking at a statue instead of a living person.

Chris got closer, trying to think of something to say or do to snap him out of whatever was happening to him. John, in full uniform, stepped out from behind Clyde. Chris couldn't believe what he just saw; there was no way John was behind him the whole time. It was like he just appeared behind him. John stood a step behind and to the right of his husband and stared at Chris with a blank look at his face. As if he was some random stranger, not his friend.

John smiled, not the plastered on grin his husband had, but a malicious grin. A grin that delighted in what was coming next. That's when John pulled out his gun and aimed it at Clyde, who still never moved. Chris did the only thing he could think to do; he charged at Clyde to save him. But he felt like he was trapped in slow motion and running through molasses. Chris was helpless to do anything except watch as John squeezed the trigger and watch Clyde fall to the ground, dead before he hit it.

John then turned his aim toward Chris, the baleful grin still fixed to his face. Chris skidded to a halt and ran the other way. Chris ran as fast as he could, but he still felt trapped in molasses. Behind him, he heard the sound of gunfire echoing around him. He saw a bullet fly past him. It left the same pulsing red heat streak in its wake the car did earlier. Another bullet went past him, same heat streak.

Chris made it around a corner, but instead of the street where his house was, he now found himself in an open field. The grass all around him was dead, brittle, the color of hay. Like there hadn't been water in this place for years. Where did the rest of the neighborhood go? He had no time to think about that now as his attention was drawn toward a group of women doing a pagan dance around a bonfire in the field mere feet away from him.

They were all dressed in tattered rags only just wrapped around their chest and hips. Their bodies had red, orange, and yellow body paint streaks and splashes on their arms, legs, and torsos. They all wore tribal masks depicting an angry fire deity of some kind. As they circled the massive fire, their bodies gyrated and whipped about with abandon. There were no drummers around, yet the sound of pounding drums was everywhere. Chris could only stand there and watch as the women continued their primitive dance around the flames.

After a minute or so went by, all the women stopped. They all slowly turned to face Chris. Then, displaying military-like precision, the antithesis to their wild Pagan movements just moments before, they all walked to the side of the fire and stood in a straight line, side by side. They continued their unflappable group stare at Chris. Chris was paralyzed by uncertainty and fear. Why were they staring at him? What the hell was going on?

Then, as John had appeared behind Clyde, the women parted in the middle and revealed Lucy standing there. She was wearing a bright red low cut ball gown with a slit down the side going up her leg. Her hair was up in an elaborate and elegant bun. She also stared straight at him, her lips curled into a seductive smile and began walking toward him with serpentine fluidity. The lipstick on her lips was as red as her dress, and the closer she got, the more he realized her eyes were the same color as well.

In any other circumstances, the sight of his wife wearing such an outfit would have delighted and excited him, but now he was afraid of her. Fearful of whatever it was she had planned for him. He didn't want her to come any closer but was powerless to do anything about it. He could stand there, quivering, silently begging her to turn away, to leave him alone. When she reached him, she put her hands on his face, as if to comfort him, then gripped him tight.

"Give me a kiss, handsome," she said in a low inhuman growl.

She pulled his face to her, and he felt her tongue snake into his mouth. Then he felt it go down his throat, down his neck, into his chest, and curl around his heart. He tried to scream and push her away, but her grip on him was like a vice. Then he felt her tongue get hotter and hotter. He felt it begin to sear his flesh and melt his insides. That's when he was able to scream.

Chapter 9

Chris woke up with a start. He sat up immediately and looked around. It was morning. He was in his own bed. The fan was still blowing cold air onto him from the bucket of ice Lucy had set up for him the night before. He was alone in bed but heard the shower going. The ice looked fresh. She must have refreshed it before she got in the shower.

Chris laid back down in his sweat-soaked sheets. He tried to take deep and steady breaths to calm himself. The remnants of the nightmare he had fading away from memory. The feeling of dread the nightmare caused wasn't fading as fast. It was just a dream, it was just a dream, it was just a stupid fucking dream; he repeated to himself again and again.

A knock at the door startled him out of his chanting. Who the fuck was at the door, he wondered. Chris got out of bed, and though he was already wearing his gym shorts, he put on a white tank top. He started to wonder if he was truly awake, or if this was the start of another nightmare. He headed toward the door, expecting it to fly open to reveal some hideous monster at any moment.

He opened the door to reveal a uniformed repairman standing there. The guy was balding and a little overweight, already had sweat forming on his face, but seemed harmless.

"Hello sir, I'm with the AC company here to take a look at your unit," he said.

Chris stood there for a moment staring at him, trying to decide if this was for real or if his mind was playing tricks on him again. He kept waiting for him to turn into something, to disappear, his eyes to start glowing red. The only thing the poor guy did was start looking very uncomfortable under Chris's intense stare.

"I'm sorry sir, do I have the wrong address?"

Chris shook his head. He wasn't dreaming, this was reality, and this is what he had needed for a while. Lucy was right to want him to seek treatment. He couldn't keep living like this.

"No, no, you're fine. This is the right house. Took you guys long enough, though," Chris said.

"I do apologize sir. We've been having a lot of units go out with this heat, we've been pretty backed up."

"Yeah, I'll bet. It's in the back. The gate should be unlocked."

"Excellent sir, I'll get started right away."

As the repairman headed around the house toward the unit, Chris shut the door and turned around to see Lucy wrapped in a towel peeking around the corner.

"AC guy finally show up?" she asked.

"At long last."

"Better late than never. I'm going to get dressed and start researching some options for you."

Chris nodded. He hated the idea of going to see a head doctor, but he had just considered it a real possibility that an innocent repairman could have been a monster. He knew he had to do it. It wasn't fair to his wife, his job, or himself. He had always been a stable guy. Was it the heat? Was it really so bad it was cooking his brain?

Chris wondered for a moment if the shadowy creature he had been seeing was real. If it was real, why him? Why was it harassing him? Chris had never been a religious man, but he never begrudged anyone's beliefs either. Did he piss off some entity he didn't even know about? No, no, that's ridiculous, he chided himself.

Chris glanced in the bedroom and saw Lucy sitting on her side of the bed, wearing her usual "too hot for clothes" outfit of midriff tank top and underwear on the laptop surfing the web. No doubt looking into possible doctors and facilities for him. Chris smiled a bit; he loved his wife so much. She always did take care of him. He'd have to do something big and romantic when all this was over to make it up to her. She'd insist he wouldn't have to do any such thing, but Chris knew he had to anyway. Maybe they'd finally take that trip to Ireland she kept fantasizing about.

"Hey, you want something to drink?" he asked.

"Yeah, some of that sweet tea we have would be great."

Chris headed toward the kitchen and poured himself and Lucy a cup of the tea they kept in the fridge. He started drinking his right away as he walked back toward the bedroom. The cold liquid felt great running down his throat. For a moment, he remembered in his dream how his insides were burning from Lucy's demonic tongue. He shook his head; it was just a dream, it was just a dream, it was just a fucking dream!

After setting her cup of tea on her nightstand, he sat down next to her on his side of the bed.

"Find anything?" he asked.

"Got a couple of places that look promising, I need to find you a doctor too."

Chris felt like a failure. He was becoming something he promised himself he'd never be, a burden. Chris could try to convince himself this wasn't his fault. No different than any other kind of illness. Sometimes folks just got sick; some people get a sinus infection, others hallucinate. As much as Chris tried to rationalize all of this, somewhere in the back of his head, he was so certain he had failed. The thought had an iron grip on him.

"Hey, you home?" Lucy asked, her voice snapping him out of his thoughts.

"Sorry, spaced out for a second," Chris responded while

shaking his head.

"Good news, I found a doctor who takes our insurance and can see you as soon as Tuesday."

Chris nodded, and so it begins, "That's great, babe. Thanks again."

"Hey," Lucy's voice going from triumphant to tender. "We'll get through this."

Chris took her hand, gave it an affectionate squeeze, and kissed it. As he held her hand, the Chinese dragon tattoo circled around her arm and turned it's head to look at him. A hissing sound like an angry, venomous snake emitted from the dragon. Chris let go of her hand and stood up. He chugged down the rest of his sweet tea.

"Babe, what's wrong?" Lucy asked, the concern in her voice unmistakable.

"Nothing, just... I'm going to get some more tea."

Chris made his way to the kitchen, opened up the fridge and grabbed the pitcher of tea and started gulping it down, determined to cool himself off. This always seemed to happen when he got warm. It's this god damned heat! It had to be! He just now realized this. The tea spilled out from either side of his mouth, but he didn't care. If he had to give himself a brain freeze, then so be it, it beat being hot.

He finished off the tea and stood there a moment, his breaths heavy. At his feet were two small puddles of the tea that managed to escape. But he felt the cold radiate through his body. He relaxed. With the AC guy doing his thing, he could last until Tuesday. Still, he pondered calling in on Monday. No sense in being out in the hot sun when he was like this.

"I'm okay," he called to Lucy.

He walked back into the bedroom. Lucy had remained where she was.

"Are you sure?"

"Yes, dammit! I said I'm..."

Chris stopped himself, closed his eyes, and took some breaths. Okay, now you're yelling at your wife for expressing concern over your well-being, which you know isn't good right now. C'mon man, get a fucking grip! He chided himself over and over.

"Lucy, I'm so sorry, I didn't mean..." he said.

Chris didn't realize it, but the cold liquid he just drank had the opposite effect, now his body was rushing to warm him back up. Sweat was already forming on his brow again.

"It's okay, babe, it's okay."

He heard Lucy get up, walk over to him, and start rubbing his shoulder.

"I just want this to be," Chris started while opening his eyes. Lucy wasn't standing in front of him, but a demon. It looked a lot like Lucy, but its face was cragged and decayed, its teeth sharp and pointed, its tongue forked. Its skin the color of ash. Chris could feel the claws protruding from its hand, making a mockery of Lucy's tender touch.

Chris had entertained the thought a malevolent entity was harassing him, but only for a moment. He had dismissed it then, but now he was certain. He was sure he was cooled down. He was certain he wasn't hallucinating. If he was being tormented, he wasn't going to down without a fight. Chris grabbed the demon by its shoulders and shoved it back. It fell back onto the bed.

"You stay away from me! What did you do to my wife?" he shouted.

"Babe, it's me, it's your wife, I'm right here."

The demon mimicked Lucy's voice to perfection, another one of its tricks no doubt!

"Liar, you fucking monster, you tell me what you did!"

The demon began scooting away from Chris, keeping a hand between the two of them. The filthy creature even dared to have tattoos in the same place as Lucy.

"Just leave me alone; just leave me the fuck alone!"

"Chris, listen to me. I'm going to get dressed, and I'm taking you to a hospital. I thought we could ride this out, but we can't wait. Okay? Please, just listen to me."

Chris then realized what the demon was doing, somehow the demon knew about the small handgun in the nightstand drawer. He charged, the demon screamed an unholy screech as Chris began pummeling the vile creature. He didn't know where his wife was, but there was no way he was going to let this abomination get away with it!

He wrapped his hands around the demon's throat and started squeezing as hard as he could. He felt the demon claw at him, trying to fight him off. He saw the demon reach the gun in the dresser, he pinned the creature's hand down and kept the pressure on. He wanted his wife back! He wanted his life back! This thing took both from him. It was going to pay!

Chris squeezed its neck until he felt it stop struggling, stop moving, stop breathing. He closed his eyes and let out a primal scream. He didn't know if what he did would bring back his wife, but dammit, he was tired of being tormented and harassed, and now it was over. Chris opened his eyes and looked down. It was a sight that punched him in the gut. He looked down and saw his wife Lucy laying very still, the life gone out of her eyes.

Chapter 10

Chris stared down at the lifeless body of his wife. His face gave nothing away, but his insides twisted in agonizing knots. Anguish, guilt, horror, and shock all sank their ugly claws into his heart. What have I done? This question slammed through his brain like a marching band playing their school's fight song.

The answer was clear as day. He had killed his wife. A woman whose only crime was loving him, caring for him, wanting to help him get better was now dead by his own hands. He continued to straddle her body, frozen in place, his mind refusing to acknowledge the reality in front of him.

Yet, reality was a relentless foe, an opponent that has never known defeat. Reality now demanded answers. Why did you do this? Why would you kill your wife? At first, Chris had no answers. All he knew is he didn't want to live anymore. The sight of the gun in Lucy's hand filled him with a compulsion to take the gun, stick it in his mouth, and end it. His life was not worth living without Lucy in it, and he was the one that removed her from it.

As he took the gun from Lucy's hand to put an end to his miserable existence, a small thought lanced through the cloud of self-hatred he was feeling. It was a simple thought, but it was enough to cast doubt on what he knew to be certain not a moment before. Was this his fault? In all honesty, was he responsible for his wife's death? Or was it that thing? The thing, the creature, the shadowy demon haunting him for the past few days.

It was that thing; it had to be. There was no way it could be anything else. He would never do something like this otherwise. The more he told himself this, the more sense it made. In fact, it was the only thing that made sense. Everything else fell away. This was the one thought keeping him from sticking the gun he was holding into his mouth and pulling the trigger. The most primitive part of himself that desired to live above all else clung to this thought like a snake wrapping around its next meal.

The sound of a clipboard hitting the ground startled Chris. He looked over and saw the AC repairman, scared out of his wits. He had come inside after hearing the commotion to see what happened, and now, he regretted it. He took off toward the front door, desperate to get away from the sight he saw.

Chris bolted after him, gun in hand. He saw the guy at the front door, struggling with the lock. The lock delayed his exit by mere seconds, but it was all the time Chris needed to raise his gun and fire off a round that nailed the repairman in the head. The man's head bounced off the front door, leaving a splash of blood, and then his body sank to the ground. The splash of blood on the door became a trail leading down the floor.

Chris stared at the dead body and the blood on his door. What was he becoming? This wasn't him. He had never hurt anyone before in his life. Now he had taken two lives in less than five minutes. But, he had to. He didn't want to. His wife was an accident; he just had to be given a chance to explain. The repairman had the wrong idea, and he didn't give him a chance to explain! He would have ruined everything! He would have destroyed his opportunity to explain!

Yet no matter how much Chris tried to convince himself of anything, he knew his life was crumbling, falling apart before his very eyes, and he had nobody to blame but himself. Out of the windows next to his door, he saw some neighbors come outside, staring at his house, no doubt wondering what the hell had just happened.

It would only be a matter of time before the police were called, assuming it hadn't happened already. Chris gave a passing thought to running. However, how long could he keep it up? Run to Mexico? Bullshit, that only worked on TV. It would only be a matter of time before the cops there found him and extradited him to the States. Besides, he didn't speak a word of Spanish.

Fighting the cops was suicide. He only had one option; he'd

surrender. It was the only logical option. He decided to put on his favorite music, lay next to Lucy one last time, and wait for the cops to show up to take him away. He knew he'd never get a chance to do this again. This was one of their favorite activities. On a lazy Sunday morning, Chris would put on some slow, smooth music — maybe some R&B or jazz, perhaps some ambient — it didn't matter as long as it was relaxing. They would just lay in bed all morning snuggling. Sometimes they'd have sex while snuggling, sometimes not, didn't matter, they loved their time together all the same.

He wanted one more chance to enjoy this activity, even if she was dead, it was better than nothing. During that time, he wanted to just stare at Lucy. He wanted to memorize every curve on her face, every freckle on her skin, every subtle, intricate line of her tattoos. He wanted to make sure he had a good, solid image of her forever ingrained in his mind. Then he could imagine her still alive and smiling. He supposed he could beg for her forgiveness, but he felt he didn't deserve it.

But before he could do this, he saw the sky blacken. Like a massive thunderstorm appeared out of nowhere. Chris shook his head as if he could erase what he was seeing by sheer willpower like this wasn't really happening. As if to mock his efforts, he saw multiple red-eyed shadow demons appear from the dark sky and head toward his neighbors. He watched, helpless and frozen in place from fear, as the shadow demons disappeared into them, then he saw their eyes start glowing red.

Chris felt a surge of anger. It wasn't enough those foul monsters made him kill his wife, made him kill an innocent repairman. They came here to possess his neighbors, to mock him, to revel in their victory over him. Everywhere Chris looked, he saw red eyes coming from his neighbors. They couldn't just leave him alone! Hadn't they done enough? Now they wanted to rub salt in the wound?

Chris ran to his gun rack, unlocked it, and took down his hunting rifles and shotgun began loading them. Chris was furious. He wanted to be left alone. Why couldn't they leave him the fuck alone? They already won dammit! His wife was dead, his life was over, but no, they couldn't fucking let it go and let him spend these last few precious minutes with his wife, listening to his music. They had to taunt and harass him just one more time. Well, fuck all of that!

Chapter 11

Jason Richardson had come outside to find out what was going on. So had Tony Stevens, and Ashley Jenkins. Old Ms. Clivoy down the street was already outside watering her plants when she heard the gunshot. Such a sound was not typical in this neighborhood. Sure, sometimes people set off fireworks illegally on the 4th of July and New Year's at midnight, but it was the middle of June in the morning, not a special holiday at night.

Jason was in the front lawn of Chris's and Lucy's house when the last sight he'd ever see exploded out of their front door. Chris, wearing jeans, a white tank top, shoes, and with his rifles strapped to his back and his handgun tucked in his pants, ran to the edge of his porch and took aim at Jason and fired. He was dead before his body hit the ground.

For the rest of the neighbors and Chris, time seemed to pass in slow motion. He ran down the porch steps while cocking his shotgun. He aimed at Ashley, who had started to run away, and fired. Her body was flung forward like a football player had tackled her from behind. Tony tried to put an end to this by charging at Chris, but Chris was able to pull the trigger again before he reached him.

As Tony's body dropped to the ground, the head now resembling raw hamburger meat, Chris felt a bullet rip through his arm. Chris turned toward the source of the pain and saw Ms. Clivoy with a small pistol aimed at him. Instinct took over as he pointed his gun at her, pulled the trigger, and let himself fall backward while doing so.

It was a move he had seen in many action movies, and he didn't expect it to work, yet it did. As he hit the ground, he saw Ms. Clivoy do the same as her second bullet whizzed over him, hitting nothing but air. He sprang to his feet while Ms. Clivoy stayed down and started running away. He didn't know where he was going. All he knew was now that he was running and fighting he couldn't stop. Not when the blackened sky kept spewing out those demons.

He ran down the street, not even looking where he was going. He had no direction, no plan, no guide. His mind was like a raw, exposed nerve. Forming cohesive thoughts was impossible; he could only react to stimuli — stimuli like a mom driving a minivan with her two children coming to a screeching halt in front of him when he ran into the road. His reaction was to aim his shotgun and fire until the screaming children stopped screaming. He dropped his empty shotgun and kept running.

He kept running. Despite the sweat pouring into his eyes, stinging and blinding him, he still saw shadow demons. They kept appearing. They didn't make a sound, yet he knew he was being laughed at, taunted, and humiliated. They appeared near and far, to his left, to his right. The more he lashed out, the more they arrived. Yet he couldn't stop.

He lashed out at a demon who was inhabiting a jogger. He lashed out a demon he saw staring at him through a window. He lashed out some more. He ran some more. He was aimless, desperate; he wanted it to be over, yet there was no stopping.

Chris heard the screeching sirens long before he saw them. He whipped around when he heard the police car come to a halt behind him. The sound irritated him, made him grit his teeth. He wanted it gone. He opened fire on the vehicle before the officers even had a chance. One of them managed to duck out of the way and return fire. Chris felt a bullet slice past his ear. He fired his rifle again, making the cop duck behind the car, and ran toward a nearby office building.

Chapter 12

John, once again, was sitting in his therapist's office on the fourth floor of the McKenzie office building. Despite the comfortable chair he was sitting in, he was anything but comfortable. The simple fact was he wasn't used to being analyzed like this. He wasn't used to revealing himself. Even to his husband, some parts of him were closed off. Not because he felt he had some dark and terrible secret to keep, but because he thought certain parts of himself just weren't worth mentioning.

But now these sessions were making him open those rooms he had locked up and almost forgotten about. These rooms were like abandoned sheds in the middle of a country field — rusted tools, cobwebs everywhere, the smell of mold and rat shit permeating the air.

"I'd like to pick up where we left off the last time. You said your partner gave you hope," the therapist started.

"Yeah, he did. He looked evil in the eye every day and still insisted that people aren't bad; they just need a reminder now and then to follow the rules, a reminder. That's what got him killed."

"You still blame yourself for his death?"

"Sometimes, but mostly no. It's like you, Clyde, everyone at the station, they all keep telling me the same thing. Nothing I could have done. It's just..." he trailed off.

"Go on."

"Clyde wants to see about adopting a kid or maybe asking a lady friend to play surrogate for us."

"Most people see having children as a positive thing."

"I know, but all I see is the bullshit in the Middle East, racial tension, school shootings, greed is essentially legal, just... all of it. It's all bullshit, and it's running our lives. Who in their right mind would want to bring a child into all this mess? I can't be certain that my child will be okay. Hell, I don't even know if I'll be okay."

"What do you mean? You're in good health, you have a steady job, a loving partner."

John felt himself tear up. He knew on paper he should be celebrating the life he had. Most folks would kill for such a life. He had yearned for such a life himself. To be loved, to be comfortable, to enjoy his work. He had all that, and yet here he was. He knew it would never be enough to silence the one thing he had known for a long time but had never admitted until now.

"I'm afraid I don't believe in happy endings anymore. All my life I've wanted to see good, but all I see is decay. Stuff gets made to fall apart; people are born to die. More heartbreak, more frustration, more fingers in the dam, but its already broken. And nobody gives a shit, we all just want our piece of the pie and play on our cellphones."

The therapist appeared unfazed, yet sympathetic, "Some might say if we didn't die, nothing we do would matter."

"Yeah, I've heard that too. I've read every report, essay, statistics analysis, anything I could find to assure me that things are getting better. And in some ways it is, so why can't I shake this feeling?"

Both John and the therapist were quiet as if waiting for the other to speak. The silence was broken by a gunshot echoing through the building. John's cop instincts were turned on in an instant.

"Stay here," he told the therapist.

As he exited her office, he grabbed his gun belt and fastened it. He saw some panicked people sitting in the lobby waiting their turn.

"I'm a cop. Stay in here, lock the door behind me, block the door, and hide away from the door, do you understand?"

One of the patients nodded, and when John exited the office suite, he heard the click of the lock. He was on the top floor of an eight-story building. The design of the office building could be best described as a stack of donuts: A giant cube with various offices all around the outside walls, with the center wide open from floor to ceiling surrounded by balcony rails on every level. There were two elevator shafts on the inside of the lazy circle. There were also fire escape stairs in case the elevators weren't working for some reason.

John looked over the balcony and saw a man with a rifle firing round after round into an office door. He pulled out his gun as the man emptied his weapon and tossed the rifle away.

John saw the man preparing the other rifle he had strapped to his back and began shooting. Unfortunately, he was too far away to get a clear shot, but it was enough to make the man stop firing and duck behind one of the elevator shafts.

John aimed, waiting for the man to come out from his hiding place when he heard the unmistakable sound of sirens approaching.

"Do you hear that?" he shouted down to the gunman. "You're surrounded! Put down your weapons and surrender!"

At first, silence was the only answer John got. Then he saw the barrel of the rifle aim at him and fire. He ducked just in time to see the bullet bury itself in the wall behind him. That was when he noticed a door leading to a stairway. When he saw his opportunity, he ran toward it to make his way down the stairs.

"All officers, please be advised: Suspect is believed to have entered the McKenzie office building on Bissonnet and 610. The suspect is armed and dangerous," John heard the dispatcher say over his radio.

"This is Officer Harris. I am in the building. I was already inside for one of my counseling sessions," he informed the dispatcher.

"Roger that, Officer Harris, can you confirm the suspect is in the building?"

"Yeah, I can confirm. I'm in a fire escape right now. Let me reestablish a visual on the suspect. Tell SWAT to stand down for now. There are still civilians in here."

"I'll do my best Harris, good luck."

John continued down the stairs as quick he could. He opened the door with all the caution and care he could muster. At first, he saw nothing, yet he knew the gunman was still in the building. He could see the flashing red and blue lights of police sirens all through the windows and glass doors of the office building.

John looked around and saw a nearby support pillar. He made a break for it. He flattened himself to it as much as he could. He prayed Clyde wasn't watching this on the news, yet he knew his husband was no doubt glued to the TV. He tried to peer around the side of the pillar, again, seeing nothing but an empty lobby, yet knowing he wasn't alone.

He didn't see the gunman, but he did see something else. Twenty feet away from where he was huddled, a woman was staring out of the window in her office door. He tried to wave at her, to signal for her to find cover, to do anything to get her out of harm's way. It seemed to have the reverse effect; she ran out of her office door toward the main exit.

"No! Ma'am! Stay down!" he shouted to her.

It was too late. John heard the gunshot ring out, and the woman flew to the side. That's when he saw something he thought he'd never see. Chris emerged from behind the elevator shaft, rifle raised, to look at the woman to confirm his kill.

Chapter 13

"Chris?" John shouted.

Chris whipped his head around and stared at John. At that moment, John knew what it was like to stare at a rabid animal. The mind was barely clinging to any semblance of what it used to be, but it was drenched with the disease. The two men stood there a moment just staring at each other, one in shock, the other trying to decide whether or not to attack.

Finally, John broke the silence, "Chris, what are you doing man? This isn't you!"

After another long stretch of silence, John saw Chris's face contort into anguish and sorrow, "They won't leave me alone!"

John eased out from behind the pillar, "Who won't leave you alone? C'mon Chris, just talk to me, man. How about we put our guns down and talk, okay? Can we do that? Can you tell me who won't leave you alone?"

Chris shook his head as if trying to ward off incessant flies, as tears streamed down his face, "No, no, you hate me. I ruined dinner last night."

"Didn't ruin anything, buddy, you just made it more interesting. Kept it from getting boring. Listen to me; I need you to put down your gun. Hey, I'll put mine down too. We can just talk."

"I can't, John, I can't. You don't understand. I have to make them leave me alone!"

He saw Chris look around like a wild, fearful animal searching all around for a potential enemy.

"Chris, look at me, okay? Who won't leave you alone? I want to help you, okay? But you have to put your gun down and talk to me. They'll leave you alone as soon as you put your gun down."

John kept slowly approaching him. He hoped he could talk Chris down, but he was prepared to wrestle the gun away if he had to physically.

"I want to believe you, John, I do. But I can't, I just can't."

As John got closer, he saw Chris's bloody arm, his whole body covered in sweat, and the tired ragged look on his face.

"Yes, you can. Yes, you can, buddy."

"That... that fucking thing won't leave me alone! I just want to be left alone."

"I don't see a thing, Chris. There's no thing. There's just us, just you and me. You put that gun down for me, and then I can help you, okay?"

John felt a glimmer of hope when he saw Chris start to lower the rifle he was holding. But then John saw something catch Chris's eye. Whatever it was started above him and then Chris followed it down to look John square in the eye with murderous intent. Before John knew it, Chris was raising his rifle and aiming it at him.

John leaped for cover behind a nearby couch as Chris screamed his rage and fired. Stuffing and fabric exploded around John as Chris peppered the couch with his bullets. John knew he had no choice now. He waited until he heard the familiar sound of Chris reloading, then he popped up and squeezed his own trigger. Chris stumbled backward behind the elevator shaft as his shirt began turning red, dropping his rifle in the process.

John ran from behind the couch to Chris's aide. As he rounded the corner, Chris was in the halfway position between sitting and laying against the wall of the elevator shaft. His white tank top was now red with his blood, and that blood was dripping down his body, leaving a small pool in his lap.

Before he could reach Chris, his friend pulled out the handgun he tucked in the rear of his pants and aimed it at him. John was caught flat-footed. He had nowhere to run, and his weapon wasn't raised. All he could do was stand there and wait for Chris to decide what happened next.

"Chris, listen to me. I didn't want to do that, you have to

believe me," John said, pleading for forgiveness as much as his own life.

He watched as Chris used his free hand to check the wound in his torso that was spilling his blood everywhere. He started laughing, as much as he could anyway, before the pain was too much.

"Fuck you, monster," Chris said, looking at John like he was a hated enemy instead of a lifelong friend. "You made me kill my wife, you ruined my life, and now I get what I want. You can't get me anymore."

"Please, let me bring in the EMTs, there's still time, we can still save you!"

Chris laughed at that again, "You just want to keep me from Lucy."

Before John could act, Chris put the handgun in his mouth and pulled the trigger. His body slumped to the ground, leaving behind a similar streak of blood the repairman left in Chris's house. John stared for a moment, heartbroken, and shocked. Feelings of guilt, shame, and overwhelming loss slammed through his heart and mind.

He walked in a daze toward the other couch in the lobby. As he did so, he got on his radio, knowing he still had a job to do.

"Dispatch, this Officer Harris. The suspect is down. I repeat, the suspect is down."

"Roger that," the dispatcher said.

John almost didn't hear it as he slumped down on the couch. It was but mere moments later that the lobby was swarming with cops and EMTs. Some of the EMTs tried to examine John, but he waved them off. Some of his fellow officers tried to congratulate him, but he wasn't sure how killing someone warranted praise. Some of them tried to offer some kind of solace, but there was none to be had.

John would find out later about Chris's other victims, including Lucy. John would cry himself to sleep that night while Clyde held him. The news outlets would call him a hero even though he felt like anything but. He refused all interviews beyond the mandatory statement he gave to his superiors. The talking heads and pundits had their usual shouting match over gun rights and gun restrictions. Funerals were held for the victims.

The following month, after John had been given some paid time off, something occurred to him. He went through the archives at the station and found the dash cam footage of the man who killed his former partner. He couldn't help but notice both he and Chris were shouting about not being left alone, about how "they" wouldn't stop. John brushed it off; it was nothing. A strange coincidence is all.

Though as he went out on patrol that day, he could have sworn he saw what looked to be a hooded figure with harsh, red eyes staring at him while he was eating lunch outside. He had already forgotten about it as he went home that night, a trick of the light plus this damn heat was getting to him. At least, that's what he told himself.

About the Author

Marcus Sabom is a born and raised Houston, Texas, resident. After living in Missoula, Montana, for two years he returned home and stumbled into the world of film-making, finally finding an outlet for his passion of storytelling and writing.

Inspired by the book series, "A Fairies Tale," he asked permission to write a supplement to the series, which later became the second book, "On Broken Wings," which he released in April 2017. Other books in the series, created by Rebecca Torrellas, include "In Love There's War," "Tangled Webs," and the newest book "Awakened Fire."

In 2017 he also released the book "The Good Friend." A movie from the book, directed by Sabom, is currently in production.

He has written (and directed) a number of film shorts, including "Catching Up," "Cocky Curls," the comedy "Let the Drama Begin" and co-wrote "In Extremis."

When he's not at his day job or trying to make movies, he's working on his next book under the watchful eyes of his three cats.

For more information on the series, visit www.afairiestaleseries.com.

For more information about Marcus Sabom, visit www.amazon.com/author/marcussabom.

Printed in Great Britain
by Amazon

70197939R00050